Juke Move

GRIDIRON LOVE

BREE WEEKS

LONE OAK PUBLISHING, LLC

To all those who have ever felt passed over or irrelevant.
You are seen.

Chapter One

Jacob

Every muscle aches as I lower my battered body into the ice-filled tub. I prefer the hot tub any day of the week, but if I'm going to show my young teammates that I'm just as tough as they are, I have to submit to this cold torture. I can't give them any reason to think what I already know to be true about me: I'm too old for this shit.

The first game of the season is still weeks away, but not convincing the coaching staff to let us practice without pads will be my downfall. That much is certain, and these aches and pains throughout my body are proof of that. I know full well the goal is to allow the younger players to experience the game at full speed. The game speeds up when you get to the professional level, and they need to get used to flying bodies, hard tackles, and body slams so hard that you feel it well into the next week. I suspect a few of the linebackers have ongoing side bets about how long I'll stay down. To earn their respect, I have to keep getting up.

Besides, during my 15-year career, some of the best in the business have knocked me to my knees. The kicker is, I've watched some of those guys go into the Hall of Fame. I can't help thinking that by being such a prominent target for them for so many years, I'm partially responsible for their success. No one's bringing a gold jacket for me to wear, so I make do with soaking my aching muscles in ice water instead.

A message from Coach MacDonald about meeting him in his office gets me out of the training room early. Though happy about the distraction, I'm worried about the reason for the summons. A coach calling an older player like me to his office out of the blue like this sometimes doesn't bode well. Panic and fear of losing my job begin to take over.

"Hey Jacob, how was practice today?" He offers his hand, which I shake tentatively and pull back quickly. I don't want him to know how sore my shoulder really is.

"It was great!" I lie.

With a chuckle, he asks, "And how's the old body holding up with this new crop of players?"

"You already know the answer to that question."

An amused expression crosses his face. "Yeah, I get a daily report from the trainers. You're spending a lot of time recovering in the ice baths."

I open my mouth to protest, but I realize he's right, and I have nothing to say to refute that. So, I switch tactics. "I'm sure you called me here for a reason, Mac. What's up?"

He leans back in his chair, stretching his long legs out in front of him. "You'll be pleased to hear I have some great news for you?"

"Really? What is it? I could use good news today."

"We have some very talented rookies and second-year players to deal with right now," he says as if I don't already know.

"Yeah, Mac. What about them?"

"Well, they're good. Some have the potential to be great, but they lack direction. Focus. Leadership. They're all too wrapped up in having made it to this level, and I think they're getting lost. They need someone to show them how to be a professional. So, I'm giving this responsibility to you this season. Our locker room needs a leader, and I think you're it. You're the great Jacob Corday. I'm sure you'll teach them well."

I sit upright in my chair, trying to understand what he's asking. "Coach, I've never taught anyone anything. I'm a football player. Not a motivational speaker. Besides, I'm not the starting quarterback. Shouldn't the leader in the locker room be the same guy who's going to lead them on the field?"

"He's not ready for that job. He's just as green as the rest of them."

"Look, I'm flattered you think I can handle the responsibility, but are you sure you want me to be the one to Bull Durham these guys?"

This time it's not a chuckle, but a full-fledged belly laugh. "That you even know that movie tells me you're the right man for the job. I'm not sure who's Nuke LaLoosh this season, but you'll figure it out."

"So that's it. The beginning of my retirement."

"Don't look at it that way, Corday. Look at it as easing your way into a coaching position. Someday."

❥ · ❥ · ❥ · ❥ · ❥

I leave his office in a worse state of mind than when I came off the field earlier today, though the pain isn't the same. Physical and emotional pain are two separate things. I'm well-equipped to deal with both, as I've done all my life, but it doesn't feel the same as before. This feels final. Permanent.

Shit! I suddenly hear and feel a crack in my knee joint. Here we go again. All my muscles are still sore, and now this? Seriously? I just want to spend the rest of the day lying down. Unfortunately, seeing Andy, another veteran player on the team, walking toward me, it doesn't look like my mood is going to get much better.

"Hey, Corday. We heard rumors about you taking some of the younger guys under your wing to show them the ropes. Isn't it too soon for that? Are you dead already?"

"You're just hilarious. I guess the powers that be want an entire team just like me. Better watch out. You might be the one they want me to sculpt next."

"So, does this mean you won't be playing?"

"No, I wasn't told that! I'll still play." I hope.

"Will you? I mean, with all that pain in every nook and corner of your body? Will you be able to?"

This guy is unbelievable! I know he's just kidding, but he sure knows how to touch a nerve. "Andy, you and I were rookies together. So, if you feel it's my age to retire, I guess I'll see you there."

"My knees don't crack like yours, though."

"Have a nice evening, Andy."

"You too, old man."

I feign a good-humored shrug and walk away, eager to get to the car and go home. Maybe I'll jump in the hot tub once I get there. Before I get to the car, my phone rings.

"Slick Rick! How the hell are you, little brother?" I answer.

"I'm good, man. How are you?"

"Couldn't be better."

"You're not a good liar."

How does he always know what I'm thinking? "What's there to lie about? I'm still on a team. The sun is shining. My little brother calls me out of the blue. Oh, and I have some news to share."

"Wah, wah… I'm not calling to hear your bullshit. Dannie and I have some news to share with you as well."

"You guys have some news, too? Don't tell me. Let me guess. You're getting married again?"

"Are you done? Bro. Cuz, seriously, you're just pissing me off now. Shut up and listen. We… We are pregnant!" The excitement in his voice is palpable.

"What? Are you for real?"

"Yep. You're going to be an uncle."

"I can't believe it. This is so exciting! I can't wait to congratulate you both in person. Are you going to make it to the first home game?"

"You gave us tickets, right? Of course, we'll be there. Dannie's so eager to see a live game she can barely contain herself." The long pause that follows is awkward, and I know he's trying to find the right words. "So, what's your news?"

"What? Oh… No, forget about it. It's nothing. Nothing compared to yours."

"No good news is small or big. Like ours is, of course, just massive, but I want to celebrate with you, too."

I hesitate, not wanting to be an embarrassment for him. "The coach wants me to mentor some of the younger players here."

"What?"

"Umm... yeah. It's weird, I know. Looks like I'll be getting some on-the-job training for coaching."

"I mean, it's great and all. But is this something you want to do?" Here he goes, asking all the right questions again.

"Of course not, but what choice do I have? Don't worry about it. I'll be fine."

"Are you sure?"

"Forget about it."

I hear a sigh, and I know what's coming. "Maybe it's a good thing. It's probably time for you to think about retirement, anyway. Not that you should retire now! Just that you might want to think about it. I mean, maybe it's time for you to settle down a bit, too."

Thankful he didn't say 'think about retirement' again, I say, "Slick, you know I can't settle down like you. I don't see that happening. Maybe in the future, but not now."

We chat for a few more minutes before I hear Dannie's voice in the background calling him for dinner, so he wants to hurry and get off the phone. All my depressed feelings sink in on the drive home. What a day! As I get closer to my big empty house, I see an empty neighborhood. Not a person in sight. I look around and it feels like a reflection of my life; lonely. When did I get so lonely? Do I have a shoulder to cry on? Who waits for me to come home for dinner like Dannie waits for Slick? I haven't felt so empty and hollow ever in my life. Though I'm happy for Slick,

I'm a little jealous, too. I'm not sure what happiness is there for me anymore. Everything is a blur. And I don't see a way out.

Chapter Two

Maris

B arging into my father's office is no easy feat with the eagle-eyed and petrifying Delores Phelps standing guard. I've tried many times over the years to sneak past his secretary, and I fail most of the time. There's an old saying that sometimes you're the windshield and sometimes you're the bug. I have a long history of being the bug in confrontations with Mrs. Phelps. But not today. I knew if I waited long enough for the gallons of coffee that woman drinks to work their way through her system, she'd need to go to the restroom, eventually, leaving her post unattended. Ha!

Quietly standing outside the heavy wooden office door, I check my hair and makeup. On point. I plan to set right a massive injustice, proving to him, and to the world, that it's time for him to take me seriously. Brushing off my blouse and adjusting my glasses, I take a deep breath before starting the livestream. Though I wait to actually start speaking until I'm inside the office and out of earshot of his secretary. It would do no good for her to snatch me up and send me packing before I make it through the door.

"And here we are guys, just like I promised, inside my father's off--"

My words cut off when I run straight into a massive chest. Rock-hard and gorgeous. The guy towers over me. He looks more bemused than startled, but I can't say the same thing about the other men in the room. They all, including my father, jump up at my surprise entrance and gasp when they realize I'm streaming the confrontation. I reluctantly pull myself away from the tall, dark-haired man who had wrapped his arms around me so I wouldn't trip when I ran into him.

"Maris!" my father's voice booms. "What are you doing? Turn that thing off and get out of here before I call---"

"Security? You're going to call security on your only child? You wouldn't dare!" I taunt.

"I was going to call your mother," he explains. "But keep that tone, and I'll do even worse. I'll call Mrs. Phelps."

"That old bitty doesn't scare me," I say into my phone, hoping no one can see that I'm lying my ass off. "I want you all to look around and see what a misogynistic atmosphere this place is. The only women who work on this floor are in subservient roles to these men. There's not one female department head in the entire building, and only a few female team leaders. And I, this man's own daughter, have completed every degree he wanted me to have, yet he still won't give me a position at his own company. I have come to the office with him since I was a little girl, dreaming of the day when I could walk in this place like a boss. If I came in here with a tray full of coffee or a steno pad, he wouldn't bat an eye. And I'm not even sure what a steno pad is!"

The hot guy stifles a chuckle, but the other men in the room look uncomfortable. My father's expression alternates from embarrassment to rage. David Robinson, the team's General Manager, looks at me curiously. "Are you livestreaming this, Maris?"

My father answers for me. "Yes, I'm certain she is. My daughter fancies herself to be some kind of internet celebrity."

"I have over 500,000 subscribers, thank you very much! Not quite celebrity status, but I'm definitely an influencer."

"That's incredible!" David says. I'm surprised he seems so interested. "How do I find you? Do I just search your name?" he asks, picking up his own phone. "Never mind, I found you."

"Don't encourage her, David. You're just pouring gas on the fire. As for you, Maris, turn that thing off and let's talk about this later at home. Can't you see I'm in a meeting?"

I have a hard time not rolling my eyes. "Well, of course you're in a meeting, Dad! That's why I'm here right now. I would like to take part in this meeting. As I've told you before, I'm a publicity expert with a huge social media following. I stole your phone last night and saw your notes for today's meeting." Ignoring his attempt to protest, I continue, "If you're planning a promotional tour with a player, I'm qualified to be involved. I'm asking now for your consideration to be part of this project. And remember, your answer is being recorded for posterity."

"Maris Elena Templeton, I will not tell you again! Turn that off, leave this room now, and we will discuss this later!"

David jumps up to stand between my father and me. "Could I have a word, Mr. Templeton?"

He pulls my father aside, and I watch their discussion intently. Well, as intently as I can with the distraction of the gorgeous man I ran into earlier sitting at the table grinning at me. The way he's looking at me, like he could devour me right now, makes me feel all sorts of emotions I haven't felt for a long time. I can almost feel his powerful arms still around me. If he were to kiss me now, I really would have to turn off the stream. I wouldn't want my followers to see me jump his bones. I might get arrested for porn if I streamed that!

My father nods at David and comes to stand in front of me. "Maris," he says, "I have an offer for you. One I think you'll like, but I'm going to ask you to turn off the stream right now."

David and Coach MacDonald both nod their heads at me. The hot guy, I'm going to have to find out his name eventually, still looks amused, but he also gives me a reassuring look. I glance at the screen and see tons of floating hearts. I'm not sure if they're happy because of my dad's offer or if they think the hot guy is hot, too. "Alright, friends, I'm going to sign off now to see what Mr. Templeton has to say. I'll let you all know how it goes." I end the stream and take an empty seat next to the hot guy. Thankful to be sitting so no one can see my shaking knees, I'm glad I'm a pretty talented actress and can exude confidence even though I'm scared to death. "So, what do you have to say to me?"

"Allow me," David says. "You have an impressive following, Maris, and I think we can come up with something that will satisfy all of us. You know Coach MacDonald, obviously, but have you met Jacob?" He points back and forth between the hot guy and me. We both shake our heads. "Maris Templeton, this is Jacob Corday, one of the most successful quarterbacks in the league."

"If he's so successful, why have I never heard of him before?" I scoff.

"Ouch," Jacob says. "You certainly speak what's on your mind, don't you? I like that." He winks, sending shock waves throughout my body, concentrating on the space between my legs. I try to shake off the attraction, but he's still staring, which I find altogether distracting.

"Oh, please. You haven't heard of him because you know nothing about football. And, yes, Jacob, she does speak her mind. No one has ever accused my daughter of being understated," my father begins, but David puts a hand on his forearm, asking him to back off.

"Look, Maris, I appreciate you wanting to take part in the team's success. Our meeting today was to map out some promotional activities planned for the next couple of weeks. You know, before the season starts. We didn't end the last season on a high note, and I'll be honest with you. Ticket sales are down. When your family bought the team, we wanted to start off better this year, and that's where you come in. We've planned a promotional tour, for lack of a better term, all across the southeast. Jacob and our team publicist, Max, will travel around to different cities, meeting with reporters from television, radio, and print media. But we really need someone who can tap into the online audience. Prior ownership never really saw the advantages of having an online presence. They were old school, you know. And despite trying to convince them otherwise, it never happened."

"So, you want me to advise Jacob on how to give internet-friendly interviews? Turn this big oaf into some internet savvy presence like me?"

"Not just that. We want you to go with Jacob and Max and conduct the interviews with him. Connect with people online. Give your own unique perspective."

"Bring my vast audience with me?"

"Now you get it! You'll have an assistant, of course, and we'll send you on the team bus and a very large per diem for all of you. So, what do you say? Do we have a deal?"

Chapter Three

Jacob

Mr. Templeton and David refer to me as the face of the franchise. No one has said that about me in a long time. I'm not sure how many people actually believe it, but it's flattering they're working so hard to convince me it's true. Still, I balked at the idea of this promotional tour when they first brought it up in the meeting that morning two weeks ago. But as soon as Templeton's gorgeous daughter muscled her way into the meeting, brandishing her cell phone like it was a loaded weapon, I was all in. Although, reading her emails and texts about the tour for the past few days made me consider quitting multiple times.

Slick and Dannie think it's cute. I don't. The old me would have resented it. Instead, I think it's annoying.

I do, however, think she's cute. More than cute, actually. Intelligent and exciting. Fascinating and intriguing. And cute.

I almost backed out once I started dreaming about her. When I told Slick that I didn't need a woman in my head like that, he laughed and wondered if I'd prefer her in my bed. I have to admit that I would, if she weren't ten years younger than I am, and my boss's daughter! Neither of those facts lends themselves to having a stress-free romantic relationship with her. I sure wouldn't mind trying, though.

"Are you ready for our grand adventure, Jacob?" Max, the team publicist, asks as we sit waiting for Maris and her assistant to arrive. They're already twenty minutes late, and I hope this isn't a precursor to how the rest of the tour will go.

I'm still sore from practice yesterday, and I use the free time to dig around in my bag for a bottle of ibuprofen. Despite my anticipation of spending time with a beautiful woman, the timing of this little trip could've been better. I should be on the field getting my body ready for the season, not sitting in this rolling tin can waiting for a social media influencer... whatever that is. Even after I googled it last night, I'm still not clear on the definition. I cross the small aisle on the bus to the small refrigerator just as Maris comes storming through the door, nearly knocking me over. Quite a feat, considering how much bigger I am than she is.

"I'm sorry, Jacob! Seems that I have a tendency to run into you. I hope it doesn't become a habit!"

"Yeah, me either." Between the hungry look in her eyes and the stirring in my pants, somehow, I think we're both lying. Sitting back down, making sure I'm out of her path, I pop the ibuprofen into my mouth and take a gulp of water.

"Are you hurt?" she asks, concern on her face.

"Just still a little sore from practice yesterday. I shouldn't complain. It's likely to be my last one for a while. Which, of course, means I won't play to start the season, or for the foreseeable future."

"I'm sorry to hear that. After we first met, I looked you up. My dad was right. I know little about football, but you looked pretty good on some clips I saw."

"Thank you," I say. "I wish I could get your dad to see me as something other than a publicity stunt."

"Good luck with that," she laughs. "I've spent my whole life trying to get him to see me as something other than a tax deduction."

"That has to hurt. So, what's in this for you? Why did you agree to do this, other than to gain your social media following by sticking it to your dad?"

She considers for a moment before answering me. "My dad and I have very different ideas about what my life should be. He's never taken me seriously, and I just want a chance to prove that I can do something other than just be his daughter. He paid for my education, but he doesn't seem eager to put it to good use."

"I can relate. Well, almost. I don't know how it feels to be the child of a billionaire, but I know what it's like to be overlooked. That's something you and I have in common."

Laughing and reaching for my arm, she says. "OMG! Are we bonding, Mr. Corday?"

"I think maybe we are Miss Templeton. Weird, huh?"

"Very weird! Well, if you'll excuse me, I have to go make sure we're set up for our first interview. It's going to be online, so I have to find a suitable spot here on the bus to set up. Make sure the lighting is right. Make sure we're far enough away from the wheels so the audience can't hear them. You know, all the fun social media-type things. I'll let you know when I'm ready for you."

I smile, "I'm looking forward to it." Surprising myself, I realize I'm telling the truth. Also surprising, for the first time in what seems like forever, I don't feel as lonely as I was. Hearing her laugh while she's setting things up gives me the peace I've been looking for.

I wonder if there is any way we could find our way in this world together. We're so different, she and I. Her phone is always present, it's like an extension of her hand. And her phone is way cooler than mine. An example of something we don't have in common, maybe? I keep all my notes on paper attached to a clipboard that I carry around constantly, a habit which Slick teases me about incessantly. I tell him it's comforting. Perhaps I could find something else, or someone else, to comfort me instead.

That is, if I can do that and still keep my job, which might be more difficult than throwing touchdowns. But I've never been one to shy away from a challenge in my life. I'm up for it.

Maris pops back into the living area of the bus. But she's not as happy as she was when she left. "Welp, this will not be as simple as I'd hoped. The lighting is best here, in front of these large windows, but we're directly over the wheels, so the noise may interfere with the audio. I could use my ring lights, but they're likely to move around with the motion of the bus."

Her assistant, Laura, looks as if she might cry, which seems extreme for such a minor problem. Max paces back and forth while Maris taps her fingers across the screen of her phone. None of the so-called experts has a clue what to do. After a few minutes of sitting through their silent thinking, I ask, "Maris, how long will the interview last?"

"15-20 minutes. Why?"

"Let's just park somewhere while we do the interview. We'll find a good sunny place so the lighting can be right, and we won't have to worry about the sound from the wheels or the ring lights jumping around."

Three sets of eyes stare blankly at me so long that I worry I must have said something stupid. Suddenly, Maris squeals, leans over to kiss me on the cheek, and jumps up with her hands in the air. "You're a freaking genius, Jacob! Did you know that?"

"We can pull over at a restaurant and get lunch at the same time. Brilliant idea, Jacob!" Max agrees.

"Of course! Then we won't get too far behind schedule! We'd planned to stop anyway, so we can kill two birds with one stone. I love it!" Laura grabs some papers from a file, thumbing through them, muttering to herself. "We have plenty of time to set up, and as long as we have a strong internet connection, we should be good to go."

While the three of them run around setting up everything, I touch the space on my cheek where Maris kissed me. I wonder if it's on fire.

Chapter Four

Maris

I don't know what made me think I could do this for two straight weeks. Spending time with Jacob has been wonderful, and I'm really enjoying getting to know him. But we've only been at this a few days, and I'm already over it. I think he is too. I know that Max and my assistant Laura are pretty well over it, too. They don't get along at all. And if I have to hear them bicker one more time about taking too much time in the bathroom, I think I might scream.

The interviews are going well, so we have that going for us. Although a couple went completely off the rails, at least we're accomplishing part of our mission. I'm not sure it's enough to sustain my sanity until we're done with this road trip. I've documented the entire process for my followers, and judging from the comments they post, they're enjoying my content. Laura and I spend most of our time interacting with them when we're not actively working with Jacob and Max.

And Jacob is generating quite a buzz among my female followers, which indeed are most of my followers. Odd. I don't mind my female followers crushing on Jacob much, but yesterday, a skanky TV reporter flirting with him did not amuse me.

He's been awfully sweet learning the jargon that goes along with being a social media influencer extraordinaire. That's what he calls me.

I'm reading comments when Jacob startles me by popping his head through the curtains and announces, "I'm starving. What's the itinerary say about getting lunch?"

"You'll have to check with Laura on that. She has the schedule. But if I have anything to say about it, we can stop in the next five miles. I could eat, too."

He plops down beside me, and I have to stop myself from swooning at how delicious he smells. I'm not sure what cologne he's wearing, but I want to soak in a bathtub full of it. Though I try to be cool about it.

Twenty minutes later, we're seated around the small table eating burgers and fries. "This can't be the healthiest meal I've ever eaten," I say, "but it's delicious."

Stuffing a fry into his mouth, Jacob says, "Well, I don't know about the rest of you, but I'm pretty sure I've gained ten pounds in the last three days. I'm not used to eating like this, and whatever I do eat, I usually work off during practice."

Max laughs. "You're still eating healthier than the rest of us! Don't pretend you didn't just blot the grease off your burger and fries before you started eating." Because his mouth is full, Jacob shakes his head and feigns surprise. "Yeah, we're not buying it. We all saw, dude."

Suddenly conscious of my own eating habits, I attempt to deflect. "Why the obsession with practice? You got injured during practice right before we started this trip, didn't you? Sounds like practice could be a dangerous thing."

"Injuries are part of the game. And I've had my share of aches and pains over the years. Nothing new to me. Besides, no one wants to get hurt in practice. It's just not cool. Save your injuries for the game."

"How about not getting hurt at all? Never mind about that, though. I've been meaning to tell you something, Jacob. I'm really proud of you." He raises an eyebrow at me. "For trying to learn all of my internet slang. It's absolutely adorable."

He nearly chokes on a fry from laughing so hard. "Not sure I really want to be referred to as adorable, but anytime I can return the favor by teaching you some football terminology, just let me know."

"Funny you should mention that. I've been doing a little research, and I would like to learn. It was surprising when my dad bought this team, because our family has never been huge sports fans. But I feel I have an obligation to learn as much as I can if we're going to be involved. And I want to be involved, more than just with the publicity, to understand the game, so to speak. I'd like to understand why people like it so much, but it's an enigma to me."

He stares at me so deeply I fear he might see straight through to my soul. "Anytime I can help you with that, you just let me know."

"Well, there was one interesting term I saw, but I don't really understand. Could you explain to me what a juke move is?"

Max, who previously seemed like he was not paying attention at all, suddenly becomes animated. "That's one of my favorite moves! It's really cool, Maris. It's when a guy's running with the ball, typically a running back. Anyway, he's trying to outrun the defense." He sees my puzzled expression. "They're the guys who are trying to tackle him. To get away from them, he jumps from side to side, back and forth, making each one of them miss. That, essentially, is a juke move. It's just avoiding everything and everybody. Not letting anyone get close to the football. Not letting anyone get close to you."

Laura, who has hardly said anything on the trip, says she has heard the phrase before in a different context. "I've heard of guys pulling a juke move when they're trying to avoid committing to a relationship. Kind of a dick move, instead of a juke move, if you ask me."

"No one asked you, Laura," Max growls.

Laura responds by throwing her container of fries in Max's face and storming to the back of the bus. Max picks up the fries and tosses them into the trash. With an embarrassed look on his face, he stands and goes to talk to the bus driver. I glance at Jacob, who looks adorably confused. "You don't get it?"

"Obviously I don't. What the hell just happened?"

"It all makes sense now. They're in love." He looks at me in askance, and I change my response. "Well, obviously, they are not getting along at the moment. They don't realize they're in love. But it looks to me as if Laura was accusing him of trying to avoid commitment. Pulling a juke move. Did I use the term correctly?" I ask with a broad smile on my face.

He snorts. "Well, if that's the case, yes, you did."

We sit in silence for a while, enjoying each other's company. I glance over at him every once in a while and catch him staring at me. We're growing closer together, and it both thrills and terrifies me. Max goes to the back of the bus, presumably to find Laura. He says nothing to us as he passes.

I finally break the silence with Jacob. "Have you ever pulled a juke move? In life, I mean. Not in the field. Are you afraid of commitment?"

"Wow! That's a loaded question."

"Are you going to answer it?"

"I'm afraid I haven't had many opportunities in my life to make a commitment to anyone, or have a relationship, whatever you want to call it. I've been married to football all my life. There's never been much room for anything, or anyone, else. But you never know. Things change all the time."

He leans in closer to me, and I feel my heart beat faster in my chest. So fast that I think it might just fly out of my body. Is he going to kiss me? Our faces move closer together. I close my eyes in sweet anticipation.

His phone is loud in my ear as it rings. His expression tells me he's just as exasperated as I am. I will him with my eyes not to answer the phone, but the bastard ignores me! "Hey Dannie! How are you, honey?"

I raise my eyebrows at the term of endearment for the person on the other end of the line. The voice most decidedly sounds like a woman, despite him addressing the person with a male name. Maybe it's short for Danielle. If it is a woman, that would most definitely be a dick move. Who the hell is he talking to? I don't wait around to find out. I grab the paperwork that Laura left spread out across the table and head to the back of the bus, leaving him there alone to talk on the phone.

Chapter Five

Jacob

Dannie's voice is loud and clear on the phone, but I'm still not sure exactly what she's saying. "I'm sorry Dannie. I got distracted. Could you repeat that?"

"What's going on, Jacob? You never get distracted."

Before I can stop myself, I tell her everything. "I probably should have told her I was talking to my sister-in-law. She gave me an angry look and took the papers from the table and left."

"So, let me get this straight," Dannie says with her best matronly tone. "You're having the time of your life, despite all your reservations at the beginning of the trip. You and Maris are growing closer together, and you think you're falling in love with her? The two of you almost kissed, just as I called. Am I right so far?"

"Yep."

"So why the hell are you talking to me? Why did you bother answering the phone?"

"I don't know! You think I should go talk to her, right?" I don't let her respond. "It's a good thing we're trapped together on a bus, because at least I know she can't get away from me."

"Yeah, I'm going to hang up the phone now. And Jacob, let me teach you a little something about women. The next time you're about to kiss one of us, do not answer your phone!"

I may not know a lot about women, but what I'm learning is that they stick together. It genuinely offended Dannie that I blew off Maris to take her call, and they don't even know each other. Guys don't give a shit about things like that.

I suspect I am in serious trouble when Maris spins the other way when she sees me squeezing down the hallway. She can barely look me in the eye as we pass.

Facing it head-on, I look for a way to get Maris's attention without just barging in. The back bedroom has a curtain hanging instead of a door, so there's not a place for me to knock. I stand outside the curtain for a moment, hoping the right words will come to me. They don't, but I have to say something, regardless. "Maris? May I come in?"

"To my bedroom? Absolutely not!" she says with no hesitation.

"It's the middle of the day and everybody has on all their clothes. I don't think there's anything to worry about. Let me in so we can talk?"

Silence. I don't back down. "I'm not going anywhere until we talk, and you can't avoid me forever. We're trapped in here until the next stop on the itinerary, and this thing is what, like 300 square feet? Come on, honey. We're in such close quarters I can hear you breathing, you know. It's a sexy sound, your breathing. I could listen to it all day, but I'd rather be sitting down and listening instead of standing outside this stupid curtain. I mean, it's a pretty curtain, but--"

The curtain flies open, and she glares up at me. "You don't have to be outside my curtain, you know. There are lots of other places on this bus you could be. Like way up there toward the driver. And don't call me honey!"

She makes a move toward the front of the bus, and I step in front of her, not quite blocking her path, but she'd have to step around me to get by. I throw my hands up in the air, showing that I'll move out of her way if she wants. "Please, Maris. Let's talk for a minute. I think you have the wrong idea about that phone call."

"I have no ideas about your personal phone calls, Jacob. They're none of my business, but I think I have the right to be upset when you try to kiss me one minute and then you're talking to some woman on the phone the next."

She blows past me, but I follow at her heels. Nearly knocking poor Laura down as she goes by, Maris is faster on her short but sexy legs than she looks. I help steady Laura before catching up to Maris. Finally reaching her, she turns on me when I place my hand on her elbow. "Don't touch me! I don't know who the hell you think you are, but I've had just about enough of you acting like you are God's gift to women."

"Would you please just listen to me, Maris? If you're angry about that phone call, you need to know something. That was my sister-in-law on the phone, not some woman!" I pull her aside, out of the watchful stares of Max and Laura, hoping she'll finally hear me out. "I like you. A lot! And I mean a lot, a lot. How do you not see that? I'm terrible with relationships, so I really have no clue what to do next here."

Large tears form in her eyes, which roll down her cheeks as she blinks. "So, that wasn't some girlfriend you were talking to?"

"No, it wasn't. Dannie is married to my brother, Slick. I mean Rick. Well, you'll understand once I have time to explain. They just found out they're having a baby, and she'd like to have a football-themed gender reveal party, so she wanted to tell me right away. Then, of course, when I told her what was happening with you, she yelled at me for answering her call, interrupting our moment."

"You told her about me?" She sits at the kitchen table, and I join her, inching my chair as close to hers as possible. Her face, contorted in confusion, stares up at me.

"Don't look so surprised. Yes, I told her about you. Actually, they both know about you. I told you... I like you a lot. I would like to get to know you better. Spend more time with you. Learn everything there is to know about you and tell you everything about me. Is that too much to ask?" I take her hand, bringing it to my mouth to place gentle kisses there. Her skin is so soft and delicate, the graceful bones in her hand seem ethereal under my touch. Another sudden urge to kiss her, even stronger than the one before, overtakes me. I fear that if I don't kiss her right now, I might lose her forever. I lean in close to her. My heart races so fast I think it might beat right out of my chest. Her pulse runs directly under my fingers as I hold her hand and pull her toward me. "I want to kiss you right now, if that's alright with you." I ask.

She answers softly, so softly that I think perhaps she hasn't heard me. She repeats herself. "I think that would be amazing." Her smile sends my heart into overdrive. Her mouth, inches from mine, curves into a welcoming smile. I know with every fiber of my being that this kiss is the start of something wonderful between us. With our entire lives in front of us, I bring her lips to brush against mine. My body reverberates in anticipation. Her scent invades my soul.

A sudden jolt of the bus and the sound of crunching metal interrupt our special moment. Tires screech and car horns sound off so loudly I think every car in the state is on the street with us. I push Maris to the floor and fall on top of her just as the microwave flies off the counter and lands where her head was a moment before. Screams assault my ears, but it takes a minute for me to realize that she's the one screaming, and the bus finally comes to a complete stop. My eyes follow her phone as it flies off the table above us, as if in slow motion, and lands hard on the floor beside me. I can't believe it. We just crashed the bus!

Above the horrible sounds of twisting metal, the echo of her screen cracking is the loudest of all.

Chapter Six

Maris

Jacob is pacing outside Laura's hospital room while I'm on the phone with my father, arranging for a car to come pick us all up tomorrow. Dad wants to send a plane, but Max and Laura have to stay in the hospital overnight, and we're not sure what's going on with Eddie, our bus driver. I insist on waiting for everyone to be released and for all of us to be picked up together. Dad's not happy, but it's the right thing to do.

"Maris, there's the doctor," Jacob says. I quickly tell Dad goodbye and rush to meet him.

"Miss Templeton? Mr. Corday? I released you both two hours ago. Why are you still here?"

"We're leaving for a motel soon. But we wanted to know how Eddie was doing before we left."

"The police officer said we were lucky. The section of the bus we were in at the time of the crash had the least amount of damage. He assumed that's why Max and Laura's injuries were worse than ours," Jacob explains, for the fifth time tonight.

"Mr. Swanson suffered a stroke behind the wheel as he was driving, and that's what caused the crash. While your other friends sustained injuries more serious than yours, I don't expect long-term difficulties for them. However, I'm not sure about Mr. Swanson. I don't want to speculate, but he may not leave the hospital for a while."

"I've been in touch with Eddie's wife and told her we'd bring him back to Nashville with us. You're saying that may not be possible?" I hate to think that I may have lied to her.

"Actually, that might work. We're not a trauma center here at this hospital, Miss Templeton. He's stable, but he'll likely need to be transferred to Nashville for further treatment. I mentioned that to Mr. Swanson, and he wasn't happy to hear that."

I scoff, "I'll bet not. He's probably worried about the cost. Please let your billing office know that the team will cover all his medical expenses. Whatever he needs."

"That's very generous of you. I'll let him know as soon as he wakes up. I gave him a sedative."

"Should I plan for his wife to come here, or.... "

"I have a specialist coming to look at him in the morning. Let's wait until then to make that decision... unless, of course, she wants to come tonight." I shake my head, since I know that's not what she's planning. When I spoke with her, she was desperately trying to find a babysitter for their granddaughter who lives with them. "Then, hopefully, he's well enough for transport tomorrow. If you'll excuse me, I need to get back to my other patients."

I've muted my phone, which is something I never do, because it's been blowing up with messages since news of the crash got out. My cracked screen hasn't stopped me from documenting the entire experience with my followers.

"Where's the closest motel?" I ask the receptionist, though I've tried to avoid her since she keeps scoping out Jacob. Luckily, it's right across the street from the hospital, so we don't have to wait for a cab or walk very far. I'm exhausted already, and though he's strong, I don't think Jacob would want to carry me. In another time or place, it might be fun. But not now.

·♥·♥·♥·♥·♥·

"There has to be more than one room!" I yell at the poor desk clerk. I realize I'm being unreasonable, but I can't stop myself and I'm just so tired.

Jacob takes my hand to calm me down. "It'll be fine, Maris. You take the bed, I'll sleep on the floor." The desk clerk gives us a strange look, but I blow it off. "Let's just try to get some rest. It's been a rough day."

Defeated, I follow him to the room, both of us exhausted. The room is tiny, and when I place a blanket and pillow on the floor, I notice a strange smell emanating from the carpet. I really don't want to know what it is.

I collapse into the bed, but it's so hard it knocks the breath out of me. I jump out of bed as quickly as I jumped in.

"You okay?"

"Couldn't be better. Why do you ask? Who needs the Four Seasons when we can stay in a place like this? We travel in style on this team!"

He takes my hand, guiding me away from what may or may not be a dead mouse in the corner. "Come on. Let's just make the best of it. What do you say? It'll be an adventure. You followers might get a kick out of this." He stretches out onto the floor, attempting to hide the look of disgust on his face when he gets a whiff of the carpet.

"Yeah, I don't think I'm going to be streaming anything from this place. I don't want my followers to see me slumming it." As soon as I say it, I wish I could put the words back in my mouth. He thinks I'm talking about slumming it with him. I lean over the bed to say, "You know I didn't mean anything against you, right?"

He raises up, and our faces are inches apart. Exhausted as I am, I want him more than I've ever wanted anything in my life. Could I tell him that? I don't have time to say a word, because my mouth crashes into his. The kiss is so unexpected that he doesn't respond immediately, so I pull back. "Oh, God, I'm so sorry, Jacob. I shouldn't have done that. I don't know why I did that."

His eyes darken with desire, and without hesitation, I kiss him again. With everything I've got. With everything I'll ever have. I press myself into him, caressing him. I remove my shirt quickly, desperately. He removes his in the same way. Fire rages where our bare skin touches. I know our passion will consume us, and I welcome it. Before I know how it happened, we're both naked. He picks me up and carefully places me in the middle of the bed.

"Oh, Jacob! I've wanted you since the moment we met. I have no clue why I never told you before now."

"As much as I love hearing your voice, I'm going to ask you to stop talking now." He kisses me again, giving me a reason not to talk. His hands run over my body, and the fire continues to grow.

I shift my weight, catching him off guard, which allows me to roll him over and climb on top of him. Straddling his powerful torso, I smile down at him, devious thoughts running through my mind. "What was it you were saying about me not talking? I think I might make you pay for that comment, Mr. Corday. And I'll take my payment now." I shudder in anticipation as I lower myself onto his stiff cock, both of us moaning as I inch myself down, allowing him to fill me completely. Feeling himself deeper and deeper into my pussy, he reaches up and places a hand on each breast. With deft fingers, he flicks each nipple back and forth, bringing me close to ecstasy.

I stretch myself forward, placing my arms on either side of his head. He now has full access to every inch of me, and he takes advantage of that. Thrusting his hips upward, making my ass bounce on his balls. My slickness covers his thick rod as he expertly flips me over, pushing himself between my thighs, never skipping a beat.

Every nerve ending in my body is firing on all cylinders as the warmth begins in my core and stretches its way to the tips of my extremities. Seconds before I come, he uses his powerful arms to flip me back over, so I'm riding him again. One. Two grinds and I'm done for!

Our bodies say to each other what our words cannot. I know at this moment that he is everything to me. He's my past, my present, and my future, all combined into one. If I never do another good thing for the rest of my life, there will always be this. There will always be my Jacob and his glorious cock.

I'm quickly taken to the abyss of pleasure. "I'm coming, Jacob," I say, as if it's not obvious.

"So am I, baby," he says a moment before we both reach the pinnacle of our passion. My body quivers as he gives me the gift of his essence. I push down hard, holding on to every tiny motion as long as I can.

I collapse on top of him, still shaking from the intensity of our joining. He flips me over, gently placing me on the bed beside him. I snuggle in close, inhaling his scent mixed with mine. Once my breathing returns to normal, I ask, "Happy?"

He kisses me on the top of the head as he chides me. "That's a dumb question. Of course, I'm happy. I don't think it's possible for me to be happier." His arms tighten around me, and he asks, "What about you? Are you happy?"

"I'm ecstatic. Could I ask you an even dumber question?" He stares intently into my face, nodding. "Do you think we could make each other happy again in a few minutes? I mean, after you recover, of course."

He laughs, slings himself on top of me, and says, "I think I can arrange that."

･❤･❤･❤･❤･❤･

I'm sore as I wake up in Jacob's arms. Maybe from the sex, or it could be from the jolt of the accident last night. Maybe both? He's still sleeping beside me, and contentment like I've never felt before in my life consumes me. As we lay beside each other last night before drifting off to a blissful sleep, we talked about everything. Our hopes and our dreams. We found that we have very similar values, and our bodies are definitely compatible. In fact, we were "compatible" three times.

Softly, I lean down to nibble his earlobe. That's one way to wake him up. Although, I discovered last night that nibbling on another part of his anatomy also gets his attention. He smiles as he pulls me close. "Morning, sunshine," he says, though only one eye is open.

"Good morning to you, too. I don't know about you, but I slept like a baby. I've always heard that total sexual satisfaction is very good for sleeping habits."

"Well, honey, let me make this vow to you. If that's the case, I promise to help you be a very sound sleeper for the rest of your natural born life."

Laughing, I say, "You won't get any arguments from me. But first I have to make a trip to the bathroom, and then I'm starving. What do you say we go grab something from the vending machine and walk over to the hospital to see how the others are doing?"

"Sounds good to me, babe."

I make a mad dash for the bathroom, finishing as quickly as I can. I throw open the door and nearly scream when I see three men standing in the room, with Jacob backed up against the wall on the other side of the room. "Dad! What the hell?" David and Coach Mac flank my father, looking confused and embarrassed simultaneously. I reach for a towel and wrap it around me, rushing out of the bathroom just in time to see my father punch Jacob. The big man goes down, and I stare at everyone with wide eyes. No one looks at me.

I scream, but I'm not sure any sounds come out of my mouth. Unlike me, my father is completely audible. He's saying lots of things. Amid all the tears, screams, and threats of violence, Jacob is rolling around clutching his jaw. I rush to him, but my father grabs my arm and says, "Put on some clothes. You're coming with me."

"No, I'm not!"

I see a look on my father's face I've never seen before. Sure, he's been mad in the past, but this is fury. He speaks quietly now, which terrifies me. "Yes, you are coming with me. If you don't, I will cut him from the roster and make sure he gets nowhere near a football field ever again. Understand?"

"I think he means it, Maris," Jacob says. "Go with your dad, honey. We'll talk later."

Dad walks slowly over to Jacob. He's still writhing around on the floor in pain. Dad says, "You won't talk later. You'll never talk to her again. And don't call her honey."

Through my tears, I dress quickly, knowing that the best thing to do would be to placate my father. I'll have time to talk to Jacob later, but I've never seen my father this angry before. I'm not sure what to expect. Fearing he might do something more to Jacob than just punch him, I resign myself to leaving with him.

I hug Jacob and try to kiss him before I leave, but he shakes his head and motions for me to go. Somehow, his rejection hurts worse than anything I've ever experienced in my life. I'll never forget it.

Chapter Seven

Jacob

I call Rick and Dannie to ask them to pick me up from the motel and drive me back to Nashville. Despite their multitude of questions, I'm unable to discuss what happened and why Maris left me in that room. I don't understand it myself, so how the hell can I explain it to them? Once we're home, Dannie announces, "We're staying in town until after the first game. We don't have to stay here if you don't want us to, but we're not leaving you alone while you're going through this breakup." I want to argue with her and explain that this isn't really a breakup. We were never a couple to begin with. How could we break up? The entire conversation seems pointless, so I say nothing.

I also say nothing about the massive headache I've had since Maris's father punched me. I hit my head on the table on the way to the floor. But he'll never know it hurt. I'll be damned if I tell him anything like that.

It's nice to have Slick and Dannie around, but there's only one person I want shacking up with me. And it's not either of them.

·❣·❣·❣·❣·❣·

Maris avoids me while at the facility over the next week. It kills me to not be with her, and I can't understand why she's just dropped me like this. I thought we were getting along well before the crash, and then later, our night together was spectacular. I get hard just thinking about her naked and in my bed.

Walking to my car after practice, I call Slick to see if he and Dannie want me to pick up dinner. As usual, the conversation soon turns to Maris. Despite me telling them both I don't want to talk about her, I spend an awful lot of time doing just that. "Do you think this is her way of allowing her father to calm down? He's a rich, powerful man, and he's also my boss. What was I thinking? Sleeping with the boss's daughter!"

"Yeah, dude, kind of a bonehead move."

"But it was the most wonderful thing I've ever done, too."

"Gross," he says. "I don't want to hear that. Listen, Dannie's made dinner, but you might want to grab a burger. She's not much of a cook."

"I heard that," Dannie says in the background.

"Sounds like you're in trouble, Slick. I'll let you go, on that note. See you soon." I end the call, but I can't end the voice in my head reminding me that my heart aches for

Maris. My body wants her. My mind is desperate to talk to her again. If we can just ride out the storm, is it possible for us to be together again?

For the first time in my life, I'm in a situation I don't know how to handle. I don't want to go anywhere, see anyone, or do anything. As if matters couldn't be any worse, I can't focus on practice. I continue to make stupid mistakes on the field, something I never used to do. That's always been the place where the rest of the world falls away. Not now.

The new defensive backs have intercepted all my passes, and they don't even seem to enjoy it anymore. They used to like nothing more than to harass me whenever they picked me off. Now they simply avoid me. As if they know I'm broken, and they don't want to gather up the empty pieces.

"Jacob," a voice from behind startles me. I turn to find Laura. "How are you?" she asks, but I can tell by the sympathetic look on her face that she already knows the answer to that question.

"How do you think I am? Do you think I'm alright?"

She shakes her head. "No. I have a message for you from Maris. You should understand that her father has convinced her she's a distraction for you. They've been watching your play during practice, and it's obvious to everyone that you haven't been performing well. She wants to be with you. She wants nothing more than that. But she won't interfere with the rest of your playing career. She feels she owes you that. David and Coach Mac have convinced Mr. Templeton not to cut you so you can finish out the season here on the team."

"Why doesn't he just trade me?" She hangs her head, as if not wanting to answer me. I chuckle. "He tried, didn't he? He tried to trade me, and no one would take me. No one wanted an old quarterback, especially one who sleeps with the owner's daughter. Am I right?" Her silence gives me the answer I need. "Well, that's just fucking great! Now what? Now what do I do?"

"I told you what you do for this season. You stay here, do the best you can, and get through the year. After that, I don't know what to tell you. That's the best I can do, and I'm very sorry. And so is Maris. She really loves you. She just doesn't think she's any good for you."

"So what, as far as she and everyone else are concerned, I'm persona non grata? Tell her she's wrong, will you? Would you do that for me, Laura?"

"I'll tell her, but it won't do any good. I know, because I've already told her. There isn't much I can do if she won't listen. I'm really sorry about this. From what I've seen, you've tried to live the right way and take care of people. You don't deserve this misery. Neither of you deserves it. Goodbye Jacob. Take care of yourself."

She kisses me on the cheek and pats my shoulder as she leaves me standing there, hopeless and forlorn.

·♥·♥·♥·♥·♥·

For the first time in my life, game day cannot get me out of the funk I've been in since Maris left me alone in that motel room. The coaches and my teammates avoid me. Even Slick and Dannie have kept their distance. The home crowd cheers for me when my number is called. They've supported me since the accident, and that's the only good thing to happen recently. The team wants to honor Eddie, who is still struggling, and they've arranged for his family to be on the field at halftime.

The publicity tour kept me from practicing for two weeks, so I'm not in game shape and struggling to concentrate on the game.

I'm suspicious when I catch Coach Mac and the quarterbacks coach staring at me. They're smiling while looking over game notes on their tablets. I've always preferred a clipboard, but whatever. Mac motions for me, and I reluctantly go find out what he wants. "Feeling up to making an impact this season, Corday?" he asks.

"What? Of course not! I'm not game-ready. You know that," I protest.

"We're professionals, Corday," he snapped. "You're ready to play or you're on the practice squad. Got it? Huddle up."

Not having much of a choice in the matter, I retorted, "What play do you want me to run?"

I can see the glee in the linebacker's eyes when we break from the huddle. He's going to eat me alive. I call the play, and the center hikes the ball to me. The game moves fast, but I've done this a long time, and I find my receiver heading straight for the end zone. I remember three things after the ball leaves my hand. First, I feel the crunch of a 350 pound man throwing me to the ground. The pressure was almost the same as the bus accident. Second, I lift my head and watch the ball hit my receiver right in the numbers and see him run in for the score. Third, I hear the roar of the crowd celebrating our overtime win. Then, suddenly, the world goes black.

Chapter Eight

Maris

Mom watches me from across the table, making me uncomfortable. "Darling, you've hardly eaten a bite. I asked the chef to prepare falafels specifically for you, as I know you love them. God only knows why."

I push the plate away, glaring at her and pouting like a child. "You said this would work, and it hasn't. Jacob's hurt. Daddy still hates him. And I'm still miserable without the man I love."

"Maris, you're going to have to trust me a little while longer. I know that you've been miserable, and I'm so sorry about that. I don't enjoy seeing you like this, despite what you thought when you were a teenager. You told me the hardest thing you'd ever done in your life was to send Laura to deliver that message to Jacob."

"And I was mistaken. Watching him go down in that game and knowing I can't be there for him has been the hardest thing. I can't show my horror in front of anyone, because I can't let on that I've been trying to deceive Dad, Jacob, and everyone else. You know, when you convinced me to take this path, I thought you were crazy."

"Yes, I know. You yelled and screamed at me, accusing me of lying to you when I told you I was on your side. But I see how much Jacob means to you, and I only want your happiness, darling. Trust me. I know how to manage your father."

"If that's true, why did he attempt to trade him?" I scoff. "We're lucky no other team was interested or he would have been gone. Unless, of course, you 'managed' that too, Mom." She meets my accusation with a smug smile. "What? Are you telling me you had something to do with that? How? How did you prevent other teams from trading for him?"

"You don't know the half of it, dear. The real problem is that your father actually wanted to sell the team just to keep you and Jacob apart. That would have been a terrible resolution."

"Oh, God! I can't believe he would do something like that. He worked for years to buy this team. How did you stop that?"

"It was really simple, darling. There were a handful of teams that made inquiries about both Jacob's trade outlook and the possibility of buying the team. I simply made a few phone calls of my own, to the wives of the owners, explaining the situation."

"The situation?" I ask, my tone dubious.

"Yes, Maris, that you and Jacob are in love and that he might not want to play for another team if it means he has to leave you. Perhaps he would prefer to retire. One simply doesn't know."

"And that worked?"

"Well, that, and I might have mentioned that your father was only trying to control the narrative because he's a pompous, self-righteous ass. Believe me, dear, the wives, girlfriends, and daughters of billionaires are quite familiar with the concept of men behaving that way. I'd be willing to bet there are more than a few of us whose fathers tried to stand in the way of true love."

"Thank you, Mom! I'm sorry I ever doubted you. With Jacob's age and injuries, I'm sure another owner would cut him immediately. As I used to say when I was a little girl, I want to be like you when I grow up." I hug her as I start to leave the table, but a thought enters my head and stops me dead in my tracks. "Wait a minute. Does that mean what I think it means? Did Grandpa try to come between you and Daddy before you were married?"

The smug smile returns, and I wonder for a moment if it ever left. "Before and after. Suffice it to say that I'm familiar with your plight, darling. In fact, it was only after you came along that your grandfather stopped praying for a divorce. Now, off with you. I have a charity function to attend before the game tonight, and I have to read my speech."

She dismisses me with a nod, and I leave, knowing I've been in the presence of greatness.

·♥·♥·♥·♥·♥·

"What puts you in such a good mood?" Laura asks when I return to my office after lunch with Mom. "I thought you'd resigned yourself to gloom and doom for the rest of the season."

"Oh, that... Well, I just had lunch with my mother, so I'm happy now."

"Maris, that makes no sense. Your mother drives you crazy, worse than your father does. How is that a good thing?"

"She just has a way of fixing things, especially things I didn't even know were broken. It's amazing!"

"If you say so. Back to business, I suppose. I pulled the analytics from the team's social media accounts like you asked. You were right. Jacob's interviews attracted a lot of female followers during the promotional tour."

"So, what does that tell you?"

"That girls like hot guys? We know that, right? So, what's the point?"

"I'd like to have something I can show Jacob. The data shows guys are more engaged with my personal social accounts when I talk about the team, and girls are more engaged with the team account when Jacob is involved. Combined, he and I have an enormous impact. The guys turn up for me, and the girls turn up for him."

"So, you want to convince him to work with you next year, if he retires."

Nodding, I say, "Exactly. I want to spend as much time with him as I can. This seems like the perfect solution, if you ask me. The toughest thing I've done is stay away from him. I've been trying to convince him and others that we're not meant to be together."

"I still don't understand why you're going through with this subterfuge. Why not just tell him how you feel and what you want?"

She's right, if it could only be that simple. "After this season, Jacob's contract is ending, so there's no reason for us to be apart after that. But Dad was right about one thing. I am a distraction for Jacob. We've all seen his practices. It's like he's phoning it in. And we know his head wasn't in the game when he got hurt. He has to focus on the game, and nothing else, or he risks serious injury. We've already seen that. I can't let him ruin the rest of his career. Not when it has meant so much to him. I'll make it up to him somehow, after he finishes playing. Until then, this is between us girls... you, Mom, and me."

"Alright. Makes sense. So, what's next?"

"I understand playing on Monday night is a big deal for some reason. I still don't know enough about football to really understand why, but I'll take everyone's word for it. Tonight's a big game. We play our divisional rivals, and everybody tells me that is significant too."

"I wonder if there is a football wife for dummies handbook somewhere," Laura says, sounding more brilliant than she could ever know.

"I don't know, but that sounds like a fabulous idea."

Chapter Nine

Maris

The stadium is rocking... literally rocking... as our team takes the field. While I've been to a game before, I've never seen anything like this. The players seem to feed on the energy our fans are supplying them, and I surprise myself, and Dad, by smiling at him. "You look lovely tonight, Maris. I like our team colors on you, but this is a bit more of a casual look for you, isn't it?"

"This is what you're supposed to wear to a football game, I think. Right? Not the suit and cocktail dress like you and Mom are wearing."

"Oh, please," Mom says, lifting her glass high in the air. "If I'm drinking a cocktail, then the dress is appropriate. Though you do look lovely, dear. I especially like the words 'Go Team' you have written on your cheekbones with an eyeliner pencil. Nice touch."

Dad and I grin at each other, which is nice. I've always had more in common with Dad than with Mom, and it's fun to feel like we're getting a bit of our relationship back. Though, if he ever finds out what I'm doing, I doubt he'll want to talk to me again.

The game starts and before I know what's happening, our crowd is booing our own team because we're down 14 points. Dad has a worried expression on his face, though he's making a valiant effort to hide it whenever the network cameras point to us.

I'm also watching the network feed of the game on my phone. I have subtitles on, but it's not picking up exactly everything the announcers are saying. And, of course, I can't tell the tone of their voices without hearing them, so I have no idea if they're saying positive or negative things about the team. Though, I'm not an idiot. There isn't much positive to say about the way this game is going.

Despite my better judgment, I send Laura a quick text and ask her what the announcers are saying on the broadcast.

When she replies, I glance over at Dad, and I decide he looks miserable enough already, so I won't share it with him. We may be in for a long, unhappy night.

The game gets worse the longer it goes on, though the score stays the same. Even my limited knowledge of football tells me that this is not a pleasant situation.

The halftime performers barely escape with their lives when some in the crowd throw hot dogs and cups of beer at them. They must be furious to waste their beer like that. I wonder as the third quarter starts if we're going to have trouble leaving. With this unruly crowd, you never know. I hear Mom ask Dad if we should leave now to avoid any nastiness directed at us as the owners. He shakes his head, glares at David, who's sitting beside him, his face bright red, before returning his eyes to his players on the field.

Suddenly, the crowd erupts into a sound that I'm not familiar with, and it doesn't sound good. I've been trying to pay attention to the game, and there's a lot to follow. But I do know when the players gather around a man as he's lying on the turf, something bad has happened. Some of them are standing close by, while others are kneeling in prayer. Someone's hurt.

My mind immediately goes to Jacob, but with relief I remember that he's not playing, so it can't be him. I'm not able to tell who it is, and it takes a moment for the stadium announcer to inform everyone that the starting quarterback is down. The reaction of the crowd seems to suggest that with him down, so go our chances for a comeback.

A hush comes over the crowd when an ambulance comes onto the field. As it drives off with our starter inside, all eyes in the stadium are on the backup quarterback. Well, all eyes but mine, because I'm watching Jacob. He's talking to the backup QB, and it appears he's trying to give him a pep talk, though I can't tell for certain. The other guy looks terrified, and although I think I probably would be too, I can't stop thinking that he shouldn't be so scared. This is his job, after all. He's supposed to come into the game if the starter goes down. Makes perfect sense.

It starts off well enough. The crowd cheers with each first down, and it's not long before we're in the end zone. I begin to think maybe, just maybe, we won't be murdered on our way out of the stadium. When I turn to look at my father, I'm happy to see he's actually wearing a pleasant expression on his face. Maybe things are looking up for us after all. The other team huddles up and tries to match our scoring drive. Just two plays into the series, we intercept. The crowd is on its feet as our guy runs to the end zone for another touchdown! A few minutes later, the other team kicks a field goal and goes ahead by three points.

As time ticks off the clock, the excitement of the crowd is palpable. When we have the ball, they're as quiet as a church mouse and are as loud as a jet when the other team does. With less than five minutes to go, we're still three points behind. The fans are electric! It's as if they're living and breathing with every snap of the ball.

Two minutes to go. I'm watching the scoreboard and the jumbotron is flashing the word 'DEFENSE' repeatedly. It's enough to give a person a headache. Though I'm still learning the game, I admit this is pretty exciting.

We stop the other team on 3rd down, and they line up to punt. Dad says, "I understand they have a pretty good punter." Whatever that means. I listen to the crowd and watch as the ball goes out of bounds at the 4 yard line. David and Dad give each other a high five, so this must be a good thing.

"Jacob once told me that our field goal kicker couldn't kick his way out of a paper bag. With where the ball is now, does this mean we have to go 96 yards if we're going to win? Because no one wants to depend on the kicker?" Dad doesn't look at me, and neither does David, but they both drop their heads. I guess that means I'm right. My eyes dart to the game clock... 57 seconds and forever to go.

The guys line up for the next play, and the crowd is silent. Even all the way up here I can hear the QB call the play. "What did he just call?" David asks, seeming like he's talking to me.

"I don't know. It sounds like a bunch of made-up words to me," I answer, though I'm not sure he heard me.

"It's an audible. He called a run play."

"What?" Dad exclaims. "We have 96 yards to go in less than a minute, and he calls a run play?"

Before either of them says another word, every player on the field seems as if they're moving in unison. All their guys go forward, and all our guys go backwards. Toward the end zone. Suddenly, several of them fall on top of one poor guy, and the crowd groans.

"What happened?" Mom asks. "Did we score?"

"No. We did not," Dad scowls. "But the other team did. It's a safety!"

The sound of whistles permeates the air as the referees pull all the guys off the pile. One of them puts both palms together over his head, like an Egyptian. "What's a safety?" Mom asks.

"They tackled our quarterback in the end zone, so they scored two points. Now, even if we get into field goal range, we can't win. We have no choice but to score a touchdown."

"Who is that man writhing around in pain on the ground?"

I even know the answer to Mom's question. That's our quarterback. Our back-up quarterback. And Jacob is his back-up. Jacob is going to play, after all.

Once again, the crown silently watches an injured player come off the field. At least he didn't need an ambulance.

Movement on the sidelines catches my eye. Jacob is throwing the ball to another player as coaches stand around watching. Everyone looks nervous... Jacob, the other players, the coaches, the crowd... especially Dad and David.

As the field clears of medical staff helping with the injured player, I move to stand behind Dad as the man I love runs onto the field. Dad looks at me and says, "I know you wouldn't expect me to say this, but I've seen Jacob Corday win games in tougher situations than this."

"You're right. I didn't expect that from you. He's a good man, Daddy. Just give him a chance. He'll take care of me."

"If you really love him, I'll back off. After all, between you and your mother, I haven't stood a chance, anyway. Seeing you walk around as if everything has fallen apart and your mother barely speaking to me, except to yell, has changed my perspective. He makes you happy, doesn't he, sweetheart?"

"Happier than I've ever been in my life," I say, tears filling my eyes faster than I can say the words.

"Happier than when I got you the pony when you were seven years old?"

"Well, let's not get carried away. I'm not sure anything could top that." I laugh.

"Alright. You win. I won't stand in your way."

I hug him harder than I've ever hugged him in my life.

The sounds throughout the stadium are a mixture of people cheering and loud music. Some in the stands near our box are singing along, others are talking to each other with worried looks on their faces. Still others are praying as Jacob runs onto the field. A player from the other team says something to him, and he responds by giving the guy a menacing look. I'll have to remember to ask him later what that was all about.

He takes control of the huddle and play resumes. It's like watching an orchestra. Everyone is in the right place. Every player runs the right route, every player catches the ball, and within just a few quick plays, Jacob has our team in scoring position. Even the crowd is keeping time with the music Jacob's deft hands are producing.

We take our last time out, and I lean down to Dad, asking, "Is this what you were talking about when you said Jacob had pulled out a comeback in the past?"

"No," he says flatly. "I've never seen anything like this in my life!" He turns beside him to wink at my mother. "If we come back and win this game, I just may kiss Jacob myself!" Mom rolls her eyes at my father, but the smile that's plastered on her face lets me know everything is going to be just fine. Just like she said.

The crowd is on its feet, including the ones here in the owner's box. We're not only on our feet, we're holding hands. The sheer will of every person in this stadium directed toward Jacob and the rest of the team is enough to convince me; he's unstoppable. When the ball finds the receiver so close to the end zone, we can smell victory. You can hear a pin drop and then a deafening moan. No one expected the receiver to be knocked out of bounds before scoring. The crowd grows unruly as Jacob runs off the field for a quick conference with Coach Mac.

It's 4th and goal, the ball on the opponent's 2-yard line. With three seconds left in the game. I wonder, along with everyone else in the stadium, what the coach will do, what play will he call.

I watch as Jacob runs back onto the field from the sideline. When the team lines up, Jacob is further back than he normally is. I look at Dad and David for an explanation, but they both look as confused as I feel. Suddenly, a smile breaks out on David's face, and he says, "Shotgun!" He glances at me and says, "You see how he's not lined up directly over center? He's behind the line about five yards. That's called the shotgun formation. Maris, get ready to watch your boyfriend do the impossible."

A chill runs over me as the crowd erupts again with excitement. They cheer and chant his name until the official sets the ball on the field to start the countdown for the last play. This is it. One play. One moment.

The center snaps the ball, and I immediately know Jacob's in trouble. He looks confused. Players run everywhere in opposite directions, but no one looks back to him or can shake his defender so Jacob can throw him the ball. The clock shows :00. Jacob still has the ball, but there's a Mack truck of a guy running straight to him. If the other guy reaches him, not only is the game over, but I worry about Jacob's safety. He's that big. He could squash him like a bug!

I want to cover my eyes with my hands, but I owe it to Jacob to watch him work his magic. With one fake move to his left, he twists around to his right, and the big guy flies past him as Jacob runs straight into the end zone. I smile, immediately remembering a conversation with him back on that bus a few weeks ago.

So, that's a juke move.

Hearing the crowd chant Jacob's name, I waste no time running down to the field. I outrun security, who apparently don't know who I am, because they try to stop me. I rush onto the field, along with what seems like every other person in the stadium tonight, and head toward the man I hope is my destiny. Somehow, in that sea of humanity,

Jacob and I find each other. He picks me up and slings me around like I'm a rag doll. I kiss him as we're still spinning.

"That was incredible!" I say when he finally puts me down.

"What? The kiss or the game?" he asks slyly.

"Both!"

"I'm so glad to see you," he says.

"I'm glad to be seen." Reporters flock around us, edging their way into our space. Neither of us cares much. We're just so happy to be together. "I have so much to tell you, but all of that can wait. Because right now, I have two questions for you, sir. What did that guy say to you when you ran onto the field? You looked at him like you wanted to murder him."

"Oh, he just told me I wouldn't get my pretty boy moves past him. What's your other question?"

I smile widely and take a deep breath. "Will you marry me?"

He answers me, but I barely hear him. I'm too distracted by the kiss that comes soon after. When we part, I look at the scoreboard and see our faces plastered on the jumbotron.

The message says, "She proposed to him. He said yes."

Epilogue

One Year Later

Jacob

Retirement at age 36 isn't so bad, especially when you have not one, but two alternative career paths waiting for you. When the season ended last year, I realized I'd achieved everything I'd wanted in my football career. I'd won a championship to bookend my playing days. I shared the first one at the beginning with the family I was born with. My last one was last year, and I shared it with the family of my choosing.

I thought long and hard about it and decided, though football would never be out of my blood, I'd had enough of the physical pain. I'd had enough of all the fame and fortune, and now, I just want a simple life. Unfortunately, when you're engaged to Maris Templeton, there's no such thing as a simple life.

Those two career paths I have, well, one of them makes me crazy, but I love her, so I do it anyway. I never thought of myself as a social media kind of guy, but it makes her happy, which makes me happy. So, once a week, we join forces and talk about what's going on with the team on a livestream. It makes me laugh to think that I didn't really know what that was until a year ago. Now, it's a huge part of my life.

The other career path, well, it's a little more me.

"Morning, Jacob," Coach Mac says as we enter the facility together. "Did you have time to watch the film of our new guy?"

"I saw it after the livestream last night. He's impressive, although he's a little greener than I'd like for him to be."

"That he is. As the team's new Quarterbacks Coach, I know you can whip him into shape in no time. He reminds me of you when you first started out, although he's a little rougher around the edges than you were at that age."

"Wow!" I say, shaking my head. "You think he's that rough, do you? I didn't have a clue what was going on back then. I was so lost trying to learn the playbook, I could barely keep my head above water."

"That's not how I remember it. Even as a rookie, you were head and shoulders above everyone else. You've always been an old soul."

"Oh, don't tell him that, Mac," a lovely feminine voice says from behind us. "He already thinks he's too old for me. If he thinks he's that much older, I may have to get him a wheelchair for our wedding."

She kisses me and shakes Mac's hand in greeting. "Did you know I have socks older than my bride-to-be, Mac? She thinks I'm joking when I say that, but it's absolutely true. I probably even have the receipt somewhere in the house to prove it."

"That's another thing we need to discuss, Jacob. No one keeps paper receipts anymore." Shaking her head, she says, "There's so much I need to teach you about being a respectable young person instead of a grandpa."

Mac laughs out loud. "Well, that's why you two are perfect together. You complement each other. That's what life's about. Now, if you'll excuse me, I have a meeting with your father, Maris. I'm hoping he's not going to tell me I'm about to lose my best new coach for two weeks on another publicity tour right before the season starts."

"Oh, I hope not either. Although, I wouldn't know anything about that," she says, beaming.

"Alright, well, off to face the music, I guess," he says as he leaves. "Wish me luck."

"So, my love," I say, pulling her closer to me, "do you have any insight about this meeting? Is there going to be another publicity tour this year, hopefully without a bus crash?"

"I don't think so. At least if he's planning one, he hasn't told me about it. Besides, I think I can keep you busy on social media and other interviews without us having to go on the road. I have lots of plans to beef up your online presence." She stands on her tiptoes to kiss me, but I give her a little help by grabbing her ass, lifting her up to meet me.

"Oh, good. I've been so worried about my online presence." I spin her around and put her back down, laughing.

She takes my hand and says, "What would you say about skipping out of here for a while? Since Mac is in a meeting, you have some time before you have to meet with the team, right?"

"Well, I think I could arrange that. If you don't think upper management will think I'm shirking my responsibilities."

Laughing, she leads me toward her private office. "I might have some pull with upper management. It'll be fine."

The End

·❤·❤·❤·❤·❤·

Sign up for my newsletter and be among the first to learn the latest! You'll also receive a free story.

https://www.subscribepage.com/j9h4o1

·❤·❤·❤·❤·❤·

Slick and Dannie's story can be found here:

As a Dirty Sinners prospect, I have to prove myself. Prove that I'm loyal, dedicated, and trustworthy. I'm loyal and dedicated to the Sinners, but some may question my trustworthiness. Men who keep secrets don't seem to last very long around here. Though my secret is nothing that will harm anyone, I'm still living in the danger zone.

To my surprise, the Sinners think someone else is keeping secrets, and it's my job to stay close to her. I've been ordered to keep tabs on Dannie McFarland, and I don't mind that task at all. What the Sinners don't know is that the beautiful library clerk has been on my radar since she first arrived in Haven. I have to make her mine, but will she bring me to my knees first?

Welcome to Haven, Tennessee. This small town is known for its wild times, alpha men and the Dirty Sinners MC—a group of rowdy hellraising bikers who don't have a problem getting their hands dirty in order to do good. Crime, passion and the forbidden temptation of love will push them all to the line.

·♥·♥·♥·♥·♥·

Read what's next for Max and Laura:

A second chance, secret baby, short story romance **Laura Murchison**:

When I fell in love with Max, I knew what I was getting. He was straightforward, honest, and passionate about everything. Despite his good points, he was a hard man to pin down on the subject of commitment, though I knew he loved me. He simply didn't see the need to talk about forever, or at least that's what he said. I thought I was fine with that, but the more time we spent together, the more I wanted the fairy tale. You know, marriage, kids, white picket fence... the shebang!

My mother taught me to be kind, and I've tried to live up to her teachings. Kindness means considering the other person's feelings before my own. Always do the right thing. Avoid anything that may cause harm to someone else. Max never wanted anything for the long haul. So, when he told me he was taking a job with his brother... a job that required travel across the country for months at a time, I let him go. I gave up my own dreams so he could pursue his.

After he left and I found out I was pregnant, I wanted to tell him. But, I knew if I did, he'd come back to live a life he didn't want. Be a man he didn't want to be. I couldn't do that to him, so I said nothing. I was being kind.

<u>Max Kershaw:</u>

Laura meant everything to me, but I was only kidding myself. I knew that one day she'd realize that I wasn't good enough for her. She lived by a code, and her kindness wouldn't allow her to tell me what we both knew: she was out of my league.

Because my childhood was filled with loss, I've never been able to bring myself to look past the moment. If I could, I'd lay the world at her feet, but I knew I couldn't do that until I could prove my worth. I thought going to work for my brother's nonprofit would get me there. The organization was born out of our grief, and I'd hoped it would make me the man she deserved.

I knew she'd lived her own life while I was out trying to find mine. Things wouldn't, no couldn't, be the same as before. But if I could convince her to let me explain, I'd have a chance.

But now I'm staring at the face of the little boy who looks just like me, and I didn't know he existed before today., I think maybe we both have some explaining to do.

You first met Max and Laura in Juke Move (part of the Gridiron Love series.) Find out what happened after the big game!

More Books by Bree Weeks

<u>The Men of The Double Down Fitness Club</u>
<u>(6-book series)</u>
This series is available everywhere, eBook and Print!

<u>Loving His Workout</u>

<u>Loving Him Again</u>
<u>Loving Him Secretly</u>
<u>Loving Him Madly</u>
<u>Loving Him Ultimately</u>
<u>Loving Him Completely</u>

<u>We've Only Just Begun (6-book series)</u>
<u>Feels Like the First Time</u>
<u>I Want You to Want Me</u>
<u>Some Kind of Wonderful</u>
<u>Somebody to Love</u>
<u>Dream On</u>
<u>Take It To the Limit</u>

<u>Thankful Hearts (4-book series)</u>
<u>The Trouble With Hello</u>
<u>Love Out of Time</u>
<u>An Inconvenient Flame</u>
<u>Role of the Heart</u>

*United For Love (Series Starters - Loving His Workout, Feels Like the First Time, and The Trouble With Hello)

<u>Mending Broken Hearts (3-book series)</u>
<u>Splintered Hearts</u>
<u>Slivered Hearts</u>
<u>Shattered Hearts</u>

<u>Not the Good Guy Series - with Kyra Nyx (3-book series)</u>
<u>Of Wicked Things</u>
<u>Of Broken Things</u>
<u>Of Lost Things</u>

<u>Collaborations and Stand Alones</u>
<u>Cracks in the Windshield</u> - part of the After I Do series
<u>Beginner's Luck</u> - part of the Get Lucky series
<u>Love Half-Baked</u> - part of the In Praise of Older Women series
<u>Sweet Child O' Mine</u> - part of the 80s Baby 2 series
<u>The Widower Takes a Wife</u> - part of the May December Romance series
<u>Summer Savory</u> - part of the Mountain Ridge Resort series
<u>Love's Faithful Vow</u> - part of the Endless Obsession series
<u>Juke Move</u> - part of the Gridiron Love series
<u>Slick</u> - part of the Dirty Sinners series
<u>The Taste of Kindness</u> - part of the Vices & Virtues

B ree Weeks writes steamy short reads that may just make you blush. She believes in love at first sight, the power of a good story, and that college football and a good HEA are the greatest things ever.

She lives just south of Nashville, Tennessee, with her husband and their dogs. When she's not writing, she loves to connect with her fans, cook good old-fashioned southern food, and spending time with her grandchildren.

Connect With Bree

Facebook: https://www.facebook.com/BreeWeeksAuthor/
Instagram: https://www.instagram.com/breeweeksauthor/
Twitter: https://twitter.com/bree_author
Website: https://www.breeweeksauthor.com/